OLD BLACK FLY

JIM AYLESWORTH

Illustrations by
STEPHEN GAMMELL

Henry Holt and Company • New York

To my brother Bill,
a legendary swatter of flies,
with love. —J. A.

Henry Holt and Company, Inc.
Publishers since 1866
115 West 18th Street
New York, New York 10011

Henry Holt is a registered
trademark of Henry Holt and Company, Inc.

Published in Canada by Fitzhenry & Whiteside Ltd.,
195 Allstate Parkway, Markham, Ontario L3R 4T8.

Library of Congress Cataloging-in-Publication Data
Aylesworth, Jim.
    Old black fly / by Jim Aylesworth;
illustrated by Stephen Gammell.
    Summary: Rhyming text and illustrations follow a mischievous
old black fly through the alphabet as he has a very busy bad
day landing where he should not be.
    [1. Flies—Fiction. 2. Alphabet. 3. Stories in rhyme.]
I. Gammell, Stephen, ill. II. Title.
PZ8.3.A9501 1991 [E]—dc20   91-26825

ISBN 0-8050-1401-2 (hardcover)
10 9 8 7
ISBN 0-8050-3924-4 (paperback)
10 9 8

First published in hardcover in 1992 by Henry Holt
and Company, Inc.
First Owlet edition, 1995

Printed in the United States of America
on acid-free paper. ∞

Old black fly's been
buzzin' around,
buzzin' around,
buzzin' around.
Old black fly's been
buzzin' around,
And he's had a very
busy bad day.

He ate on the crust
of the **A**pple pie.

He bothered the **B**aby
and made her cry.
Shoo fly!
Shoo fly!
Shooo.

He coughed on the Cookies
with the chocolate bits.

He drove the **D**og
nearly out of his wits.
Shoo fly!
Shoo fly!
Shooo.

He frolicked on the **E**ggs
for the birthday cake.

He licked up the **F**rosting,
for goodness sake.
Shoo fly!
Shoo fly!
Shooo.

He danced on the edge
of the **G**arbage sack.

He got sweet **H**oney
on his dirty back.
Shoo fly!
Shoo fly!
Shooo.

He hid in the Ivy
by the kitchen sink.

He stole some **J**elly
as quick as a wink.
Shoo fly!
Shoo fly!
Shooo.

He played on the **K**eys
by the kitchen door.

He lit on the **L**ist
for the grocery store.
Shoo fly!
Shoo fly!
Shooo.

chocolate
eggs
apples
olive oil
honey
milk
salami
jelly
noodles

He lapped up the **M**ilk
in poor kitty's bowl.

He nibbled on **N**oodles
in the casserole.
Shoo fly!
Shoo fly!
Shooo.

He crawled in the spills
from the Olive oil can.

He pestered the **P**arrot
on her stand.
Shoo fly!
Shoo fly!
Shooo.

He snoozed on the **Q**uilt
on Gramma's bed.

He rode the red **R**ibbon
on her head.
Shoo fly!
Shoo fly!
Shooo.

He sniffed the **S**alami
that sister sliced.

He ran around her Teacup
once or twice.
Shoo fly!
Shoo fly!
Shooo.

He slept on the stack
of clean Underwear.

He played on the **V**ase
by the velvet chair.
Shoo fly!
Shoo fly!
Shooo.

He dozed on the **W**indow
in the summer heat.

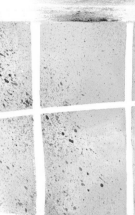

He made a little **X**
with his front feet.
Shoo fly!
Shoo fly!
Shooo.

He buzzed about the **Y**arn
in Mama's lap.

He landed on her table,
flap flip flap.

Zzzzz **Z**zz!
Zzzz **Z**zz!
Zzzzzz.

Old black fly's done
buzzin' around,
buzzin' around,
buzzin' around.
Old black fly's done
buzzin' around,
and he won't be bad
no more.